BEYOND THE PORTAL: FROM WITHIN THE MYSTERY STONE

Michael A. Susko

AllrOneofUs Publishing
Baltimore, Md & Huntsville, Al

While every precaution has been taken in the preparation of this book, the publisher assumes no responsibility for errors or omissions, or for damages resulting from the use of the information contained herein.

BEYOND THE PORTAL: FROM WITHIN THE MYSTERY STONE

First edition. April 18, 2022.

ISBN: 979-8201873004

Written by Michael A. Susko.

For those who imagine other worlds and find treasures of the soul.

We are going on an extra-dimensional adventure, using imagination as a tool. The imagination is typically seen as a human faculty, but it may also be a faculty that opens a real door or portal. That is, imagination can take you to places that exist. You may think you can only imagine things that are made up and cannot be believed. But you can imagine realities––that is, if you hyper-imagine, in which you become immersive, in which you are exposed to deeper truths and the understructure of reality. It is possible, if you spend time beyond the portal.

So I ask you to enter this doorway or portal with me. I am opening mine, but you can accompany me. It has been called in literary circles, the capacity to "suspend disbelief." Lack of faith tends to shut the imagination portal. A major task in life is to become free of empire thinking, its artificial boundaries, and not just listen to sources within its loop.

For to imagine truly, you have to be free. The irony is that even someone bodily confined can soar and escape the walls of their cell. All done without a key. The only way to stop this is to depress or diminish the brain, through such means as others may contrive, such as heavy drugging or electrical current. But even then, the human spirit finds ways to triumph.

Let us prime ourselves to begin the journey. We can enter a partial trance state and go to somewhere beyond, a place which has its own landscape and set of rules. Does this land exist? Yes, it does...*beyond the portal.*

CHAPTER ONE

I have asked a companion to be with me. It is a half skeletal figure, found on a stone from the Shenandoah. I know the figure well, having studied it for months, knowing every turn of incision, every dint impressed. Some can reasonably hold it was made by a person hundreds of years ago, but some claim differential weathering, plow marks, or tumblings of a stream. It doesn't matter how the stone was marked, whether its agency was nature, accident, human intentionality, or spiritual forces. For I will still ask these forms of unknown origins to accompany me as a spiritual companion, who will show me mysteries by opening a portal.

We all need to be saved by something or someone beyond ourselves. Even if it is a humble stone with markings of unknown origins, I will accept this gift. Perhaps we would expect this saving force to be a beaming, multi-colored light, such as created in space from two colliding galaxies. No, for now it is a humble stone which is micanized, possessing thin mica flakes on its surface which flash light, amid the crystalline heartstone shapes. So let there be light; there is always light. We see because there is light. We don't just see a thing; we see the thing in light, which possesses a certain temperature, intensity and hue. Light is the hidden third companion in our world.

My companion is waiting to join me, and it is present here, if only thinly at first. He or she does not yet have a name. An unusual thing about this companion is that it's a twinned being, having both sexes overlapping. It can be, however, in some manifestations of itself, a male, and yet in other instances, a female. Perhaps, too, it can operate as a singularity, with both sexes conjoined.

Finding its name is important, and I think I have the beginning of one: *Heartstone.* For although the being appears encased or haloed by mineral energy around it, the heartstone shapes made by dozens of dints reveal the shape of a spirit being. Its quartz crystalline nature reflects whitish-gray, yellow, and hints of green. It absorbs much darkness.

Heartstone speaks of soul, which penetrates every being in the universe. For without soul, *fielded energy connected to a deeper source,* there would be no world, nor physical manifestations at all.

"You have found and named me," spoke the being. "But I am not confined to this stone. It offers clues about me, true. It is only a starting point for us to adventure beyond the Stone. It is a portal and invitation for you to enter."

"To what land would you take me?" I ask. "Is it to your time of origin, or the future of more advanced consciousness, when this work will be but a plaything for the young?"

At this point the being became more manifest, emerging as a 3-D figure from the Stone, enfleshing or enstoning itself into what looked like an animate doll. It held a light which was intrinsic to its being, a self-contained light which did not overwhelm or overstate itself. It was physical and soul at the same time.

"We go to where you are ready and where you need to go," the silvery being replied. "It's a place where your being is bathed in living light from the other dimension."

"Yes, I would like to go there. Take me then."

"You do not arrive there all at once. The passage has tests along the way. The full soul world does not appear so easily."

"Let us begin then."

"Look at me, observe and see what comes to pass."

I unshielded the original stone and gazed upon it. Something new came into view.

"I see a reptilian-like head curled with a chameleon body spiraled in birthing. It lies below your form."

"Yes, we birth when we enter a portal and various creatures appear. For the creature world is part of the realm beyond. They are elemental forces, pre-souls as it were. It is the mystery of beginnings."

"Does this reptilian being join us?"

"You have guessed correctly. Hold this creature in your hand and let it birth."

I did as asked and held the newly found. It was delicate and small enough to be held in my palm, but I sensed it could become much larger.

CHAPTER TWO

When I looked up from the creature, I noticed the skeletal being was now human sized and taller than me. It had a sleek, whitened look as if it were all bone, yet it was proportioned as if it wore flesh. Its face was unique, for it had an avian look, with a beak-like nose, large black pupiled eyes, and a head whose back displayed ecstatic projections, whether hair, feathers or partly both.

"Who are you?" I dared to ask. Although I had named the being and felt it to be my companion, there was still something unnamed. It came to me that this being was still veiled by *mystery*, leaving much of its identity hidden. I did not know its deeper name. And even if I were to know this other name, the being would not be fully known or understood.

Meanwhile, the reptilian being had uncurled, having fallen from my hand and enlarging in a short space of time to the size of a large dog. *Birthing is foreshortened in this world,* I thought. Things *come to their intended shape quickly.*

Despite this speed of events, it felt I had entered into a type of time that was timeless, while the reptilian being experienced the more organic passage of time.

I saw, faintly at first, but then more clearly, gossamer wings unfolding from the back of the chameleon-like creature, and I realized it too was from another domain. I thought of the hybrid creatures who were guardians of the ark, which held the sacred Presence. Here in this domain, I realized that normal biological constraints no longer applied and that creatures could merge into unlikely combinations, so long as the underlying principle was upheld.

Having viewed this winged creature, my gaze turned to my companion being, whom I saw more clearly as one of whitened bone-essence, a spirit-bone being linked to soul and elemental earth. Heartstone was permeating with mystery, an essence which could not be fully described or limited, whose revelations would continue to come as long as one kept interacting with this being, who was continually birthing from this Stone.

"Where do you wish to go?" asked Heartstone, the sudden question being unexpected. Then I saw a rainbow pattern of winged energy unfurling from the bottom half of the Stone. Perhaps I should have been taken aback by the further contradiction of wings coming from a boned shaped being within stone, but it seemed natural and effortless, happening as a matter of course.

"Climb aboard," Heartstone invited, gesturing to the winged reptilian creature.

It seemed as if I had only wished it when I found myself atop this creature and rising into the world above. "Where are we going?" I asked, and I was surprised that the creature beneath me answered, "To the First World."

Its answer only raised more questions. It implied there was more than one world here, and they were sequenced by some principle I had yet to discover.

Although the creature had wings, they seemed to be tailing in the wind. Our forward motion was made, it seemed, by a thrusting chevron shape which could break through dimensional barriers. Powered by some unknown source, I wondered if it was connected to the interior of the Stone. The mystery of inter-dimensional movement was held by this geometric shape, whose fielded energy tapped into a source.

The winged creature followed the wake of this shape, like the lead bird that broke the wind for a group in formation, and more, providing the propulsion.

"What shall I call you?" I asked, trying to exert some control.

"You may name me," it replied unexpectedly.

I realized things in this world did not give up their true names easily, as had been my experience with Heartstone. No ready or particular name came to mind, but its lizard like dimension, crest and array of color led me to say, "Chameleon, you are then."

The creature-being was pleased at my response, for I sensed a faint smile come to its face, which was not so much reptilian as a being prior to mammals or reptiles. Here I sensed a potentiality of consciousness had become actualized by the connection it had with the abstract form that was breaking through the dimensional barrier ahead of us.

I always imagined that dimensions were simply crossed by stepping through a singular portal and not by an extended journey. One can only experience the entrance to another dimension and not direct it. Perhaps a journey was necessary, I reflected, to prepare myself for the strangeness that was coming.

CHAPTER THREE

We land, or rather we remain suspended, but I sense we are there. We are in the First World where birthing of inchoate forms swirl and create dozens of more forms that shape as you view them. It is a world of coming to be, of not yet fully being, of taking shape. Your guess is as good as mine for what is there. I see an eagle form for one, outlined there. Is it really there? Its head rises upward toward the skeletal being, and below its wings and body it dissolves into oval spiral forms which are ever making. It's faint, lightly abraded, a precursor being of something that will become more definite as it rises from this world. Then the beak of this form reverses and becomes a head crest, and a miniature of the larger skeletal companion, a somewhat angelic-looking form appears to be an unborn version of the larger one. That its unborn self would be present in this lower world is remarkable and leads me to wonder if we carry our unborn self within us.

Out of this matrix comes an eagle or proto human-avian form, a faint etching of the being's prior life, reminding me of folklore, of an infant carried by a stork. As I am suspended, I look downwards and see my legs elongated and without feet, going to the bottom of this world, as this Stone has expanded to human proportion.

On the other side is yet another avian form, more defined, but also rising from this region of birthing, as if a second stage or companion to the first. More than one head presents, depending on my looking and what gestalt forms. The whole form goes upward as well, and instead of being a lighter abrasion, it is darkened with splotches and an outline. Its upward thrust is given not only by its wings but by a swath of red which leads upward and to a larger and new extended head.

That birds or bird forms are present in a watery, amorphous realm would seem to be a contradiction and not expected in any world. Yet, who am I to question? The Stone is my teacher, not curtailed by my expectations.

"Where do we go?" I ask again, putting the question to all these forms.

Heartstone answers. "We go to the spiral of life's making."

We enter into a barely made-out form, the cusp of an oval. Descending, we follow a spiral which leading to the interior of the stone. What is inside cannot be read or viewed, as it's a hard matrix known as quartzite, earth's most abundant mineral, formed from liquid rock, magma that cooled when it surfaced from earth's interior. Yet, it is more than a mineral which is hidden from view, more than the stardust from which it ultimately came. In this case it is penetrated by spiritual being, an alliance of Stone and Spirit which presents a mystery. This spiral is taking us deeper into this mystery, to reveal to us how things begin.

Such a mystery cannot be directly seen or heard. Rather, it can be remembered, as you yourself were once in an interior, a watery realm from which you birthed. You must go back to that point of your life cycle to experience beginnings and realize how that which was invisible becomes manifest.

It starts with a spiral form of expanding cells, becoming a spiral fetal form, which becomes the infant which unfolds from its mother. We go back to that first spiral, that first unfolding.... our first sense of movement; it is like the chevron of our skeletal being!

Into darkness, we feel pressures around us as our being extends. We move outward, our being expanding. The *spiral* is unfolding, the first becoming of who we are.

If only for a moment, I was the being of my first movement, then jumped in awareness to being a full adult being ingrained in stone. Crystals sparkled all around me, suffused with spirit, and I called out to my winged chameleon friend. Grabbing its crest, I am brought out of Stone into a thinner medium which I could breathe, for it seemed I had not done so while inside the stone. I am birthed...

CHAPTER FOUR

No sooner had I emerged from the Stone's interior than I was caught in an amorphous realm, whose birthing nature had become replaced by threat. A perilous sense to things prevailed in the deepening color, the unformed nature of forms which began to buffet me. They took shape as a large monstrous beast, one with an ever shifting face. *What is this thing?* I wondered. I sensed that though it presented as exterior to me; it was also a part of me, a shadowy side I had only half glanced before. The conjunction between birthing and peril recalled my own life and how the entrance of new life did not occur without its own drama.

"Speak to me, being," I asked, wanting to gain further clue as to what I was facing.

A low rumbling sound emitted, and the monstrous thing showed another face, this one larger and more primeval than the first. It was half fish, half beast with a human glint to its eyes.

"Why do you obstruct me?" I asked. "Why would you keep me from doing what is good?" I sensed this monster's mission was to diminish me, to keep me from accomplishing what my life's task.

The beast did not answer, and I wondered if it did not have the capacity for speech. Yet, I sensed primordial pre-words which held emotion. These I could not translate, other than the impression whatever force this being represented, it must be overcome.

How do you slay an amorphous beast that shape shifts in front of you? I had no weapon, such as a sword, and I sensed one would only slice through a substance that would reshape. Maybe, too, it would only grow larger, fueled by hate. At a loss at how to respond to an enemy I must dispense with, and having no way to do so, I asked again.

"Who are you? What name do you go by?"

I heard a deep syllable that reverberated throughout the First World and into my being. It revealed who it was, though I had not the tongue, nor voice to repeat the sound.

It came to me that the only way to conquer this force would be to merge or overlap with my being, while keeping my consciousness, so I might know my enemy more intimately. I used myself as a sword and cleft into this enemy to see what I might discern. I entered and for a few moments I am now this beast, this creature which presents different faces to the world.

I see things I have never seen quite so clearly, so starkly. My failings taking shape around me, like all of my warning dream images dangling before me. There was no quick turning from them, nor any distraction that could ease this pain. Yet somehow the pain, as long as I looked, diminished some, for the act of facing these painful failings brought a measure of healing.

At this point the beast creature disappeared, and I was suspended in the amorphous world, alone. It seemed the skeletal anthropomorph too was but a distant memory, and I was left to fend my own way. How long I lay suspended I do not know, for it was a space where I did not remember my past, nor project my future. I only felt the immediate pressure of these fluid waves against my body, as if I were en-wombed.

Then I saw a shape above me, a sinuous shape dipping into these depths, spiraling as if surrounding a moon. It glowed as a beacon showing the way out, and I reached toward this opening. As I approached, the way constricted and something wound itself around my neck, and I could not breathe.I knew I would die unless I reached this lunar shape, unless this strand around my neck was cut, and I was lifted out of these depths. My first act of coming into the Second World was marked by a perilous passage, for I almost died when I was born.

I came to life, and a breath happened, and the sinuous form became a passage into the world above. If someone escapes peril at this stage, it is a portent of yet other deaths and rebirths to happen. As to what cut this umbilicus, and I do not know, but I saw a white tool dabbed with magenta held in a hand, which I took to be the anthropomorph's.

The sinuous form itself was a portal and passage into the domain I had come, and it led upwards into a new realm. This new realm was filled with movement and wounds, but it gave life.

Then I saw below me the source of movement from which I had come, a winged-shaped design pierced in its center, leaving a haloed mark which showed red. Here was the center of gravity to the anthropomorph, to the Stone, and to these Worlds. Here was the pelvis whose sacrum marked the center of things, which kept balance to movement and was the place from where things birthed.

I had already passed from this shape and was being led to something that cut deep into the sinuous form. It was an oval marked with a central spot which glistened red and which had feathering designs radiating from around it. Around this oval, a swath of dark red surrounded its lower portion. I knew I was being called to yet another death and passage, which would reveal a deep mystery of the Second World.

CHAPTER FIVE

I am in the world between the knife and the wound. The wound ahead is an opening, revealing the next stage of my coming of consciousness. Walking along the top of an undulating hill, I notice the sinuous being has become the landscape, and that I had landed in a place that looked like earth. Implausible as it may seem, I am drawn to talk to the form under my feet and the landscape responded.

"Why is there so much pain, so much blood in the world?" I asked. "And why do you lead me along a great wound?"

"One is called to break into worlds and go into something new," answered the being. "The passage is not easy. When you first enter, there will be a period of restful motion until the next world presents."

Perhaps a glimmer came to me, sensing the need to break out of whatever constructed ego boundaries I had in order for new consciousness to emerge. It was like an infant struggling to push its weight forward to crawl, to move, to get to the next stage. It takes a lot of grunting and exertion that the infant has forgotten, but the parent witnessed.

We may forget the pain and the struggle, but it's present at every significant passage of our life. Call it the cross, the Darwinian struggle for existence, or the Buddhist Dukha. If we evade this struggle, shrug off the cross, we become stuck in a land where nothing changes, where we experience the same o', same o' and then, such is the human condition, we begin to regress to a prior level of consciousness.

The landscape rippled as if it were living and indeed it was this sinuous being. Ahead I saw the Oval tear in the midst of its being, and the wound that created the opening, all of which was swathed in dark red.

I stepped into the Oval, pitted with small moon-like craters, whitish gray dints with hints of green. There was one crater near the lower center, which glistened with red and looked like blood. I wondered if I should dive into it and be baptized by this blood. I wondered too whose blood this was and whether it was the sinuous being. Then I saw, to my amazement, appearing over this pool of blood, a half-skeletal shaman form. Wondering... had it come to warn me or invite me?

"Who are you?" I asked the stone a second time, sensing much remained unknown. "I have called you Heartstone, but you are something more, as much of you remains hidden."

The Being responded directly. "You have also thought me as *Mystery*. Who I fully am is for you to discover."

That the being knew my prior thought and invited me to discover its mystery affirmed a type of mutual power or connection. I felt a thrill at facing a future unknown, and one I could not predict.

Looked hard at the being, its shapes connected by threads of energy, I realized I did not truly comprehend its nature. Perhaps the closest I could come was that it was a spiritual being fused with bone. It was not angelic or human, but an archetypal force, part of the hidden order of things and which had been given to me as a companion.

The pool of blood awaited me and I realized I must dive into it, that it was another door to this portal and that beyond it lay the unexpected.

I jumped into this red pool and went into the Stone. Within its matrix I sensed the presence of the crystalline heartstone and faced an inverted version of the skeletal being, in which his light areas were dark and his dark areas, as his eyespot, were light.

"Where are we?" I asked

"We are in the land where your shadow side becomes visible."

I scanned about, but only the being was there, amid crystals that held the faintest flickers. "Where is this shadow side?"

"For now, I take on that aspect for you," it answered enigmatically.

For the first time, I looked at the being as an aspect of myself. It was me caught in transformation, half bone, half enfleshed, part light and part shadow. I looked or tried to look at it steadily, but it faded from clarity. It knew the parts of myself that absorbed light rather than give it off. It was not wrong to absorb light, but the light absorbed should be turned outwards again for others to see. When the light stayed in the shadows, it became murky and a presence slippery to others. Where was the *there*, the light in that person?

I turned to the being for help, for I sensed I could not gain clarity about this shadow side on my own. After all, this being, which could be a dimension of myself, offered a type of clarity, even if it be a half clarity.

"You are becoming," said the inverted skeletal being. "Imagine the dark aspects of yourself turning to light and let what you see as good to recede. Invert things and tell me what you see."

It was a novel invitation, to consider what we take as dark and have avoided looking at steadily as filled with a potentiality for light.

"Take one small aspect," invited the inverted being, "and see what you discover."

I took an aspect which I took as most pressing or immediate. It was a direction of energy toward the self, an absorption of energy that was kept from reflecting outwards for a wider and greater good. It was not the aspect was wrong in itself, so much as a greater good could be channeled and a bigger battle for good could be waged.

I did not know whether I should go one level deeper into the Shadow dimension or whether I should surface for air and continue my journey on the face of the Stone. I did neither, it seemed, but went through the stone to its backside. There I found a black smear, a zigzag indentation, which were plow marks, faint parallel striations, all which presented as empty and unremarkable. *A wasteland*, I thought, *an unfinished life, a land with no direction or quadrants such as a mandala would make.* Then I noticed my half-skeletal companion was gone, and I was alone and stranded.

It was night, the stone as large as a landscape. I don't know whether it had expanded, or I had become smaller. I had no idea how to go back through the stone, as no opening presented. I would have to walk to the edge of the stone and hope gravity would turn with me as I circled back to its front side. Which direction should I go? As to the stone's top was uphill and offered resistance and headed to the bottom. If I could turn the corner, I would reach the underworld that I had already passed. I thought this world was done, but it was better to return to that world, even the underworld, than stay alone on this trackless waste.

How long I walked I do not know; it was beyond the point of exhaustion. It was only me and my body, which seemed to be shedding as I continued. Whatever I was coming to, I would not be the same afterwards.

When I reached the bottom of the back side of the Stone, it seemed I would fall off. To one side, there was a dark cavern that cut into the stone to one side, which I avoided. I found an unexpected passageway, an indentation that led to a faint incision which became a road leading to the face of the Stone. My feet adhered to this path, as if they knew the way. As I turned the corner and viewed the continuing line, and I realized it was the beginning of the leg of the anthropomorph, engraved into the Stone. So the anthropomorph being, or at least the fossil impress of it, would serve as a bridge for a passage over the underworld.

CHAPTER SIX

The anthropomorph's legs were a bridge over the turbulence and unformed swirling netherworld below. I did not want to go there anymore, so I followed the boned path toward This World, which would ultimately lead to the center of this being. It held the promise of being filled with spirit, crystallizing into centering designs, in which energy was taut and directed.

For now, I followed the expanding legs upward, bridging the expanse of the netherworld. It was a depth caved into the stone which had inverted to become a ridge which I could cross, as if the Being had altered its conformation for the journey. One side was steep while the other gradually inclined, and I stayed nearer the height and the steeper angled side. For the sculptor or whoever made the original stone had directed its blows from that angle. Who was the sculptor was a question I could not answer now, but I sensed it would become apparent when I reached its face.

I wondered about the nature of the "leg," of which I was on its left side. Were the knees bent and tensed to place the anthropomorph in a state of trance? Was it also moving forward? I sensed it was both at the same time. The being was in a state of trance, which altered perception of the cosmos and which made for spirit movement. Like a dream body, it was moving in its altered state.

The legs were not the end but rather a passage, and they took me to the wing-like form which I had earlier bypassed but would now experience more directly. It was the center of movement and gravity for the whole being, a neglected and unreflected upon dimension of our being.

The pelvis contained the glowing orb of the body's center from which movement springs, and from which new life emerges. It is also the source of ecstatic pleasure, related to when two beings join.

In the center of this winged shape, which was not inverted but presented as a bowl, was another red mark surrounded by an oval. There was always a center from around which energy radiates, I reflected.

I wondered where I would go from here, for a center can place you anywhere on the landscape you traverse. Did I want to seethe face of the sinuous being, or of the anthropomorph, which were in an upper raised region. From the latter, lines radiated to designs on top of the Stone, which appeared to be the logical end of my voyage. Or, did I want to go Eastwards toward the mysterious chevron shaped which propelled the anthropomorph forward into the future?

I chose the future, to that which is birthing. For I needed renewed energy and being before I ascended into an overworldly domain. I touched the center of the pelvic form and wished myself transported.

Thrown beyond this form and to my left, I followed a wave of dark energy that went against the flow of the sinuous being. I reached the *chevron* shape and hung onto it, as it was propelled by an energy and pulled by what lay ahead.

The shape I found myself within had become inverted and was like a spaceship. Within the chevron was a cruciform form, from which the ship was controlled. Although it was propelled by an energy unknown to me, it was responsive to my thought and desire. Through this form, I felt the entire universe was available to me, and that distance meant nothing.

I began my travel into infinite realms, beyond this being and whatever creatures accompanied it. I was among stars, or rather, the world of birthing stars. For I was going forward into space among the galactic swarms and coming closer to the present, for the light of the stars had reached us was aged, having taken millions of years. Now I was close to stars that gave their first light, being among a birthing cradle of them. This fresh light penetrated the ship and myself, and I felt the immortality of my being. It was not immortality coming from me, but it came by being refreshed and renewed by this light. For without this light, I would decay into a vaporous dust, and be but an instant more before I vanished.

How can I describe this feeling of immortality? It was none other than being continually reborn and renewed, as if always awakening into a wondrous world.

No sooner had I become lost in this feeling that I found myself back on the Stone and witnessing something rising from the underworld which would undo this reality. It took the shape of a huge feline beast which sought to devour that which is birthing. Nearly hidden in the stone's corner, a deer-like animal was curled in a convex nook of the Stone. It was the place which birthed animals into the world, which this rising beast sought to destroy.

There are powers threatened by anything new and wondrous. Why anything would want to stop good presents a mystery, but I think it can be glimpsed. That which has turned toward evil and only seeks its immediate desire is pained by the good. It brings the realization of something deeper and truer which has been lost to them and is still being lost. If they have lost that, they wish others would lose it too.

I felt helpless before this rising feline, that I could do little to stop the destruction of birthing. But the half-skeletal shaman form was emerging once again from the Stone. The Chevron wing became its arm, holding a white dipper-shape which I took to be a weapon. The warrior in me arose, and I realized we must slay this beast if birthing was to be saved.

CHAPTER SEVEN

The beast had already swallowed its share of stars, which had turned to dead pumice within its interior. It now approached the birthing animal. Seeing a zigzag form on the Stone's surface, I picked it up in hope it might help in this battle. As my hand locked around the form, it transformed into a white-boned, glowing object. Somehow, it funneled the electrical energy of my being and could shoot pulses at the invading feline.

My effort only delayed the being, but by this time, the skeletal being had fully arisen to confront the feline. They faced each other and things became frozen, with no clear winner of this battle. I retreated toward the center of the stone.

I didn't make it to there, for I was caught up in wafts of smoke that came from pipe form crimsoned in magenta, mostly along its underside. I sensed this realm of mystic smoke which rose in abstract patterns would carry my thoughts and feelings to the world above.

In this arena of breath and spirit, I faced the skeletal being. It was complex, with shifting, beak-like avian elements leading into a human skull shape with a large darkened pupil. It was a map or impress of the being, not the being itself. Yet it offered clues to its mystery, and perhaps its impress was animated by its living force.

Then Heartstone appeared at my side, and I wondered at this twoness. Not looking directly at it, I continued to observe the impress in the stone. "The face is a mystery," I reflected. The face, I knew, was its own organ, an entity formed distinctly in the fetal state.

The half skeletal being responded, and the message echoed in my mind. "It holds clues to the subtle soul which cannot be seen directly."

I reflected upon this and thought about how, except in a reflection, we do not see our own face. "Yes, we are hidden even to ourselves," I said.

"In discovering the other's face, we come to know our own," Heartstone revealed.

"Our being unfolds with another," I echoed. I thought of all the time I had spent alone and wondered if otherness was imprinted deep within our own self. I dared to ask, "Is not our own soul partly other?"

"Perhaps you take on too many mysteries at once," the half-skeletal being warned. "For mysteries are layered one upon the other, and no sooner have you entered into one than a greater one presents."

"What spirit lays within me?" I asked, pursuing the question doggedly.

"The answer is not found so easily with words. You must continue your journey into the interior and experience it directly."

I sensed the central energy below in the heart of the being, but was still within the dented and curled markings of its face. The energy of its face extended to the back of the head with sharp extended lines that looked afire. Suddenly I saw another oval making for a second head. Heartstone had a hidden spirit companion, and I realized my friend was twinned with a feminine companion.

This unsuspected doubling made things more complex and complete at the same time. We may think of ourselves as singular, and so we are. Yet we can imagine another dimension of ourselves, hidden and subtle in its manifestations. As if to echo this thought, I made out two ovular lines connected the two heads, making for an intimate twinning.

I did not try to enter or discern more about this second head. Rather, I descended the neck chakra of the first being, which had its own peculiar, petaled markings.

But this second head would not let go of me so easily and called out, "Why do you turn from me?"

Turning, I looked more closely at the oval shape and saw the bare outline of features, two pupiled indentations and the outline of a smile, more skeletal like and spirit infused than nought. I wondered about this face. It was a layered face of beauty, which went deeper into a shifting variety of faces, as if all feminine forms were present in this face. The faces changed, but I sensed their beauty merge as a single face, as if the archetype of the feminine form were present. A fetal dimension was present in this beauty, as if the face were eternally young.

I realized that which is hidden may be more beautiful, more strong and more real. We don't expect a surprise at the center of things. Yet if we open ourselves, discovery becomes unlimited. That energy and beauty seeks to enter and fill our being—nay, even flood it.

I go down to the center of things, the center of the body, the site of transformation, where things and substances of earth are converted into energy so that one can move and be. Although it has complex underpinnings of organic structures which can combine the fuel in the air with the things we eat, an abstract architecture presents as well. For underneath all these workings is soul. A soul makes life, the impetus for life, and it springs from a sacred source beyond and entwined with the body. This spirit-flesh melding is one of the greatest mysteries of this world.

This reality is reflected by certain lines and lineaments of this petroglyphic impress, in which a hidden architecture provides a clue and map to deeper reality. While the microbial biome connects us to the deepest and oldest layer of life, there is also the connection to the ever-renewing spiritual source of life. The gift of life is granted us, a gift which is our personal most fundamental mystery, for why we came to be. For the spiritual world decided to manifest the person who is you. Thus, you have a deep purpose and reason for being, even if it remains hidden for much of your life. What could this purpose be in the most general way? I cannot help but think it has to do with experiencing and sharing beauty and meaning with others. This puts the universe on a path of ever-increasing beauty and meaning.

On the impress, this inner world took the form of a spiral leading to a petaled center, all contained with a double oval. Like the cell, the soul has its membrane and a center. It's a flower, or an unfolding flower at the center of our being. The structure of soul is in three dimensions, such that it could be seen as a raised mound with a temple at its top. This calls to mind the teaching we are all temples of the Holy Spirit. An immense sacredness is present in each of us, no matter how obscured or oblique that reality may appear to be.

For a long instant, I saw things from a spiritual perspective, an inversion of usual sight, where seemingly great things are small in the spirit world, and small things in our sight are great in the spirit world. This inversion, seeing things as they are in the light of an ultra-reality, is not our usual frame of reference. A person, ruling oppressively, would be quite small compared to a street sweeper who showed simple kindness to those around him. If we could truly see in this way, we would aspire to like the street sweeper, not the great ruler. Our history books would be filled with stories of seemingly small people, whose worth would equal or surpass that of emperors whose bad deeds, even their own historians, could not expunge.

In the inverted empire of the small, love and acts of love are the stuff of eternal value, not power and domination. Then the contest in this world should be to see who could be the better servant and most prolific gifter.

It was then my attention was drawn below this vessel of soul, and I saw the heart of the action of the anthropomorph. In this being's hand, a white dipper was filled with a substance that was a mystery. This was the being's gift to me and to the world, and I surmised it was a precious substance related to soul—perhaps a portion of its own spirt. It was a seemingly small gift, yet I knew its value should not be underestimated. Part of its mystery is that it will not been seen by everyone, and fewer still would be open to receiving this gift.

One other form was present, so subtle as to be almost missed, but found between the torso vessel and the gift in the white dipper. A centering design, a double circled mandala, framed a cross. This design over the abdomen of the petroglyph embraces periphery and center. Perhaps it's related to the miracle of our bodies converting earth's substances to energy that sustains and moves our being. It was an intimation of the servant world, in which less complex orders of being support the evolution of the more complex, with the more complex raising up the lesser.

"Would like a drink?" asked the anthropomorph, whose mobile form suddenly appeared next to me.

I could not refuse, though I was fearful. *I will never be the same again if I take this,* I thought. My life would become more aware and more difficult. Yet I was too immersed in this spirit world to turn down its gifts, so I accepted the dipper from the being's hand and drank.

It was clear and tasteless, yet unlike anything I had before. It felt pure, as this unknown substance melded with my being. My body became like a single white skeletal sheet. It was one with things around it, in which nothing could be excluded by dislike. This singularity of being combined with borderless inclusion was a state of spiritual love.

It was a gift, for I found it natural now to be in a state of selfless giving, rather than bounded by the closed nature of ego, trying to satisfy myself, carrying the weight of dissatisfaction with myself. It was a grace that sought the higher and greater good and made it easy to do. It required acceptance and emptying, to not be distracted by lesser goods. The ability to accept this gift should not be underestimated, for the universe continually offers this. It requires one to stop but for a few moments and become open.

"What do you see?" asked the anthropomorphic being. I looked and found it was now totally enfleshed and draped in a spiritual cloth of wings. The wings were shimmering as a rainbow, and it seemed to be a third human, a third avian and a third angel. Its finished form had become apparent in my graced state. I wondered if the being had really changed, or if I had, such that I was now able to see what had been there all the time.

"Are you ready?" asked Heartstone.

I realized that a journey, yet further, was about to begin. It would press to the edge of things not yet known to myself, things that would only become known in the future of humanity. I was invited on this journey, so I could share this journey with others at this time.

CHAPTER EIGHT

"We are going off the grid," announced Heartstone. "We will not be contained by impresses, but go beyond the Stone, which is a portal."

"Are you the portal?" I asked.

The Being did not answer directly but invited, "Come." And I rose in the swirl of its wings into a space above and beyond the Stone.

We continued this way for so long and far that I wondered if this was the destination, to be endlessly moving. The surrounding space was formless, with energy sweeping past us rather than wind. As these glimmering flashes passed, I slimmed, my body becoming streamlined and avian-like. I was becoming like Heartstone, a twin to his form.

I thought this journey was taking me somewhere, but it was more about me transforming. It was not just the hollowed bones of a bird, but into a crystalline heartstone. It felt not like the heavy substance of stone, but the bonds of the stone which I kept within me. These bonds were more real and stronger than the original crystalline rock, which made the Stone heavy.

I realized that form makes all things what they are and that substance could be shed. Yet it was not totally shed. Rather, the substance became hyper-real, its essence being retained.

I knew or sensed too that whatever form or substance I was taking was immortal, that it would not decay or pass. It would outlast the explosion of the sun in seven or eight billion years, a sun which had already "lived" a third of its lifespan.

This Elijah-like experience caused me to wonder if I had died, if I would ever return to my earthbound state, with its higher percentage of substance living under the sun.

"Have I died?" I asked.

"The death you imagine has no sway here," the being replied.

I noticed Heartstone did not answer my question directly, and I wondered if I should ask again. If the Being answered, it occurred to me its words might permanently set into motion this path to hyper-reality. I would rather leave it open for me to choose. For as wondrous as this reality was, I did not feel my time had come to permanently leave my earthbound state.

Then I gained an insight that all people were seeking spiritual reality and that many sought it through beliefs which were false. Ironically, it was the very falsity which made for a type of transcendence, an assertion they were not bound by common belief, that there is something both unexpected and more. Yet for falsity to serve as a mode of transcendence is a shaky foundation upon which to rise, and I found one reason I must return was to help deliver those who are ensnared.

I fell back into the underworld, where there are many wounds, where a mass of people are gathered like an army. How and by what power they could be tended, I did not know, but I felt asked to tend them. Then I realized I could become a conduit for power to flow from the Stone, from the anthropomorph, and from the Source beyond. This three-way melding would enable me to show some kindness and be present. I realized my small acts, like leaven, might help raise others up.

One voice spoke out of the many, and this person asked, "Why do you tarry?"

If all things have a mystery in them, so did this. Why we fail to do the good or wait so long? Is it because there is a dragon in our shadow side preventing, leaving us too wounded to act? Perhaps the answer is that doing selfless things is a mini-death to our limited self. Since deep down we do not want to die, we fear to perform selfless acts. Yet acts of love raise the world to a greater consciousness and spreads like leaven to influence many more than we expect. I had these thoughts but no ready answer in words and absorbed the comment in silence.

The anthropomorph, who could access all realms, appeared by my side. "Your own wound must go deeper, the death of your constructions be more complete for the transformation to occur," Heartstone revealed.

I did not want to die and become entombed in a stone, leaving behind only an impress. The anthropomorph had somehow already gone beyond this and would know the way.

Would I trust this being enough to travel in its wake and go to my death? And what would be on the other side of death?

CHAPTER NINE

Out of the amorphous mix of the underworld arose a double of myself, a shadowy gollum which sought my destruction. It had invaded the Stone's world from the future, it seemed. Was this the creature that would bring my death? I realized to die in this way would be ignominious, bringing a death worse than a physical death. It was death of the soul, whose fabric is torn by moral collapse.

The gollum attacked me, and I grappled with its sinewy form. I managed to wrestle it away. I am stronger than I realized, but danger was still present as others like it lurked in the background. Two lay near the first, as weak as he, but two others stood about, looking stouter and stronger. If they attacked at once, I wondered if I could hold them off.

I called out to Heartstone, who appeared. He held a spear-like implement in its hand. "Who are they?"

"They're cast-away versions of yourself who still survive," the being answered.

"Is my job to kill them, or to make an accommodation with them?"

"How you conquer them is decided by you," answered Heartstone, who receded from view.

I wondered at this choice, and I was undecided. Endless fighting with these creatures was not a good option, for it would absorb my energy and limit the good I could do. Like Heartstone said, some form of conquest was necessary.

What was it to be? Perhaps I could delay the choice. One of my failings was procrastination, and I sought a way out of the underworld, leaving behind the creatures.

Two ways appeared. A hawk form was unexpectedly present. Perhaps it could animate and serve as a way out. Also, a long plant stalk was at the edge of the stone which could serve as a path. But what of the shadowy doubles? Should I take the hand of one and rise with him?

In the end I decided to incorporate the being I fought, to integrate its shadowy form as a dimension of myself. Being tamed, closer at hand, was better than trying to cast it off, I decided. For if I declared it a stranger, it might keep coming back and growing stronger. Its energy I hoped to redirect, to channel toward humility and more ability to gift. As the shadowy being subsided within me, I soared. I wondered if this incorporation of the shadowy being gained me a transforming power, in which I could rise as an underworld hawk. A blood hue we passed through was a clue to what would come next.

I rose toward the center of the anthropomorphic impress. The oval-portal appeared like a canyon on my left, and on my right, a large thumb-like shape cut into the neck of the sinuous form. This gouge was surrounded by dark red. Once again, I was at the wound at the heart of the Stone. This time I flew above the wound to the face of the sinuous being. It was bulging, bearlike, with white haloed eyes. The central portion of the face had an incised boundary, an equal-sided triangle that ranged from its eyes to mouth. I wondered of this confluence of organic form with geometry, and whether the latter were soul lines. For a mathematical precision reveals the soul form underlying living things. That a mathematical flair is present in the universe's structure is a clue and code a message about the nature of things and the reality of a beyond. What is beyond? For that, I would have to reach the Stone's top.

I saw forms above me and a groove to follow, but I could not ascend, for the blood hue had become too thick. I was paused. I realized I could not pass through this being unless I paid it some respect or due. "Who are you?" I asked. "You rise from the underworld, where your tail is like a curled moon, but your head has two broad paddled forms which go up into the Overworld."

"I am a bridge between worlds," the Being answered. "I am that which demands sacrifice at the center of the Stone."

It occurred to me that this was a mystery the being had revealed. There is no real progress or advance in consciousness unless we embrace sacrifice. This being from which red imbued the Stone had shown by example how life sprouted from its spilled substance.

I sensed this being was demanding a sacrifice from me as well, but I did not know what was demanded, or when it would be. I did not wait to find out. As soon as I gained this realization, I was released and able to ascend.

I made my way up with the hawk through a grove which led to a giant pouch whose top was feathered. The hawk landed on the edge of this pouch, and I glimpsed down at its contents and saw it was filled with seeds of all types. *The seeds of the world* are here, I thought. They were capsules in which life had paused, waiting for the right time to come into its full, unfolded form. *We are all seeds like this,* I thought, and I wondered if my time had come.

CHAPTER TEN

I felt myself become like a seed that could grow, and I wondered what my next step would be. Would I ascend to the feminine domain of the second head and explore the patterns of the flower world above? Or should I go down to become a seed to experience the plant from root to blossom?

It is unfinished, almost omitted, work, the humble plant as a path to enlightenment. And I knew I must descend as a seed and take root in the dark earth. I had help. The female side of the anthropomorphic entity had taken me out from its pouch and tossed me down to take root.

We might think of the plant as a messy consortium of earth, microbes and root tendrils, but there is a part of a plant that is essence, without which there would be no plant. I came to that place, close to the root. It was deep at the bottom of the stone where the plant started.

Drained of my animal energy,my desires became slow and focused upon essentials, seeking light and moisture. My lower being sought moisture while my upper being sought light. I had transformed into a plant. How mystical it was, how simple and good it was, and how pleasing it was to receive the simple substances of light and water.

It was like music, the patterning of water and light, with my tendrils/ leaves reaching to maximize my access. I did not know whether I preferred light or water. For water was a substance that kept my being refreshed, giving me body so I would not wilt. Light gave me an impulse for rising and providing the fire that would keep my being going.

I rose from the root and my stalk self reached toward the top of the stone. My first set of leaves were large, one angled straight toward the oval Portal, and the other a large drooping leaf that curled around the bend of the stone. I rose further into a swirling pattern of life, a series of shoots and a leaves extended to the sun. For each leaf along the way were like steps to my rising. My being coursed upwards through the phloem, as if I were the sap, the plant's blood.

The energy started to coalesce, to come together, ready to burst into a novel pattern. At the top, it took form as a flower, a ring of petals with a center, as all radiating energy has a center. Above the flower were raised tassels, as if to adorn the flower.

Becoming a flower with its sensitive, fragile colored leaves, called petals, was an exquisite feeling. I had become beautiful and would attract many as a flower. Yet this flower would only last for so long before it would fade and go to seed.

Then I saw ahead of me a type of stair or ascending marks on the stone that would take me to the summit and to the end of my journey. The first of these designs at the end of the sinuous form. One projection of the bear-faced being could be seen as a creature itself, with a snake-like head and a three pronged design on its forehead. From this design emanated an animal light, an intensity that appeared to emit from its brain. It came to me that the brain was not the origin of this light, but rather like a plant leaf that needed light and moved toward light. There was a light reaching this brain. It was immersed in waves of *consciousness*. As the sun bathes the plant world with light, a light of consciousness is bathing upon the animal world. This light is awareness, a sense of being to which the evolution of animal life is ever stirring, toward greater and greater consciousness, mirrored in its amplified neural systems.

This light impacted the neural center, indicated by the design on the forehead of this creature, the light carrying a greater awareness than the creature itself. I sensed this light was not bounded by time, that it contained a deep awareness of past and the future to which we are pulled.

Questions were raised in my mind: What was the source of the light? Could this being reveal knowledge from the future? In the questions I sensed, the answer was already half revealed. For if the question were never raised, the answer would surely remain hidden.

As this snake form presented as a muse, I posed it a question. "Where does this light come from? Do you sense its origins?"

"The Light comes from within the Stone," the snake-headed creature answered. "It also comes from beyond the Stone."

"How can both be true at once?"

The being did not hesitatge to answere. "The primal energy of the universe existed before there were things."

It felt a great secret had been revealed, one which I could not fully wrap my head around. Yet, if true, my head would be wrapped by the flood and light of primordial consciousness.

I sensed this primordial consciousness was inherently prophetic that it knew the deep past and distant future. I asked the creature, "What do you foresee for the future of humankind?"

CHAPTER ELEVEN

"The path is on a razor's edge," the being replied. "You can go one way or the other, a path in which small deeds can make a big difference."

I wondered at this and feared to know more. Yet I was curious as to the fate of humankind and pursued. "Tell me of the two ways."

"Which do you wish to hear first?"

I wondered about this, but then the answer was obvious. "First, the bad way, for I want to end on a note hopeful for the future."

"So be it," said the creature, and I rode atop the form, lifted over the Stone and traversed the world. We arrived in an instant to places, pausing over zones of darkness where war, famine, and abandonment of others reigned. Places where children suffered things they could not understand. For if their larger world did hateful things to them, this to the child's mind must be the nature of the universe. And who would want to live in such a world? That parents and society could not or would not care for its young was a devastating hurt as well.

"Enough," I said. "Why would humankind choose such a path and expand such a path? Who wills to hurt children?"

"The fantasy of power does," replied the snake-being.

"When one is young and immature, such fantasies begin."

"Yes, when one is between child and adult..."

Such was the paradox, the world's fate being determined by adolescent fantasy. Incredible too that such fantasies were rewarded in this world, in which ill-gotten gains become ever more enticing, and that people do not reject temptations that would ruin their souls.

"Show me the way that goes toward good," I asked.

"You must ascend the stone further to experience that."

In front of me, a concavity lay between the projections of the bear-faced being. I could not ride to the crest of the stone without considering this hidden face. Its profile was beak-like and his head was adorned with a falcon headdress. I wondered what this face was doing here and its meaning, so I asked directly, "Who are you?"

"I am the hidden self," came the immediate reply. Then, as if to answer my questioning look, his words continued. "There is more to oneself that one knows, which can be continually discovered. The spirit self is ever moving into the future."

I saw the avian form as part of that future. The face was not just some trick relic descendant of the dinosaur, a jokester side of the universe, which revealed that out of all the grand dinosaurs, only this fragile kind survived. This bird-human could soar, escape the world, and reach new heights of consciousness. Every day of life is birthing new consciousness and discovery in the world, and one has to be but open to receive its coming.

"What draws us on? Is there something pulling us into the future?" I asked.

"You have perceived well," answered the avian being. "What draws us is a much greater and grander force than we can imagine or say in words. We can only experience it and let words follow. It is all things at once, a refreshing coolness, an unimaginable warmth, a light ever unfolding. It's a being whose love for you, if you felt it but a few seconds, would all but overwhelm you."

"You have told all that needs to be," I said, recalling my own past. "Why do I need to go any further?"

"Telling is not the same as experiencing. I invite you to remember your own experience, to call upon it, that it may sustain your struggle."

After that, the face receded from view, for it was only in certain lighting and by carefully looking that it was visible. From there, I moved to the second projection that extended from the haloed eye of the bear-faced being to the top of the Stone. It had a similar trefoil design as the first, and I sensed another prophetic eye, one that could see the future.

I floated over this design, then landed upon it. Sitting as a Buddha within its petalled shape, I experienced peace, a place of rest and a base before any further ascent. Above me, I sensed the future was present. Yet nothing was visible, and it felt like an opaque white dome was above me.

I rose, as if shedding my old body, slipping off me and coming to an arc above the trefoil design. A slit above me opened into the future. What I saw surprised me. The trefoil design had blossomed into greater intricacy and more varied shapes, making for a geometric garden of delights. There were no scenes, no events here, but *being* reigned. I glimpsed this for a long time. Then the door to the future closed, and I wondered if it was true.

This future must be millions of years away yet, I thought. For our world is still undoubtedly one of doing and of struggling. But this place of rest exists or will exist, one of pure being, in which we do not have to continually battle and face the tests of this world.

There were two more smaller designs within a concavity, which took the form of a thistle and a curl like an embryo. I would become as a seed again for this final birthing outward, to finally go beyond and above the Stone. This most insignificant of designs, seemingly worth only a passing notice, spoke a significance. They were spiritual seeds within my psyche, which had not yet blossomed. What were they?

I gave up, let go of this fullness of being to become a seed again, that I could birth something new from its smallest beginning. It started as humble marks with minimal shape, with the promise to blossom into something rich and complex.

"Here you will see how the small opens a door," I heard a voice say, and I realized it was the feminine head which had birthed this domain above her.

I wondered at this connection and difference between the biological seed we all once were, a single cell, to the spiritual seeds found near the top of the Stone. Were such seeds planted within our soul that would sprout at different times in our life, set to reveal novel forms and dimensions to ourselves? Have we become closed to the possibility of such new growth? Perhaps we expect nothing significantly new to happen in our life. Yet, surprise seeds are within us, waiting to germinate and to be cultivated when they are allowed to sprout.

I ascended and came to a design more full and blossomed. It had a hand-like aspect, and within the hand was an eye. I had come to another portal, one intimately connected with the feminine head, for lines reached through this head from below.

The combination of hand and eye reflected the most intricate tool of our sensation and subtle outreach of our physical being. It is also the focus of will. For where we direct our gaze and how we direct our hands is a product of our continuous will. This was more than a normal hand and eye. It was a spirit eye and a spirit hand which served as a portal, an entrance which would provide yet the fullest view of the world beyond.

CHAPTER TWELVE

I supposed this portal would take me to a land beyond the Stone, but I was mistaken. I went into the hand through the eye and found myself within the Stone. Around me were thousands of crystals, green-gold glittering, and fractaled. My being overlapped or bled into this geometry, such that my body's boundary was no longer distinct. I was one with the Stone, which was fluid, not hard set or frozen. How matter became fluid, neither liquid nor gaseous, but its own liquid crystalline form is a mystery of the universe, one that allowed my being to merge with the Stone.

At first I thought this substance was simply uniform and equally penetrated the interior of the stone, but I was mistaken. There was a Being or consciousness within the Stone which had been hidden until this point.

Its outlines took no one shape, but shifted according to my angle of view. It was anthropomorphic, yet also plant and animal, able to merge into other identities, having an essence that could manifest in different ways. This mystery within the Stone was unexpected, yet made perfect sense. All the forms manifested by the Stone had to come from a Source, and that they would come from within the Stone was a logical place.

"I am surprised to find you here," I intoned, uncertain what this entity was.

"An essence of the universe is surprise," the Being responded. "When you have closed that door and think you have captured all that is known, you have made Stones as these dead."

That our minds could kill a stone was a novel consideration. Then I sensed the Stone was more than matter, that it was filled with animate energy by the Being within the Stone.

I asked, "Teach me what I need to know to sustain myself, to not go off the track, so that I might bring the most life."

The Being responded, and the form it took seemed to be all three kinds of life. "You have asked well....If there were words which could magically lead you to always and certainly do good, I would say them. As it is, I can only point the way. Your being unfolds in the moment and you make an ongoing choice for the good."

"There must be a word, a mantra I can say, an *Ohm* to keep me aligned with what is necessary and good."

"*Love*, one could say, but it is more than a feeling or sentiment. Love's essence is found in its doing. Try to do three good things each day, things you must will yourself to do."

"Three seems too much... I rebel against doing things that feel like it's bringing death to the self."

"Then do at least one good thing... For out of that will come many things."

It seemed such a minimal request I could do and add to the total good of the world. If all the billions of persons in the world did one selfless good thing each day, how the world would change.

"How do I know which good thing I should do, for wouldn't it be easy to do a small thing?" I asked.

"A small thing it can be, but one your conscience presented to you."

I felt the light of consciousness all about me and that it was filled with requests, with needs being asked. If I permitted myself to step into this matrix, filled with needs, I would know what to do. But I held out hope the doing need not be big. One small act born out of this light/consciousness matrix would reverberate instantly around the world at a speed faster than light.

I realized many avoid light and consciousness because it's mixed with these needs and the pull of our being to respond. Although the doing was not impossible and most of the time not even very difficult, we shy from the light of consciousness because it is entwined with demands.

Then I faced the things that kept me from a full spirituality, good things omitted from my doing and my choosing/being absorbing myself in lesser goods, and I offered them up as a pearl to the universe. For I can not let these things weigh on me and stop me from my daily tasks. Each time of my failing, I will recenter my being and gather the fragmented parts of myself.

There are many such pearls scattered about the landscape of my soul at the top of this Stone. I saw it in an unexpected way, that a recognized failing is a spiritual gift and part of the progression of consciousness.

"How is that so?" I asked the Being within the Stone. "How can our failings be a part of the progress of the universe?"

"When we confide failings, we draw close," answered the Being. "This closeness becomes the pearl. In this closeness the answer lays."

Perhaps this was another mystery revealed to me, and I blessed the Stone with its attendant consciousness for having come into my life.

I still wondered, "How were the markings made on this Stone? Were they from differential wear of an exposed Stone in which the elements chanced these forms? Or were they markings of a human who went through a vision quest experience? Or, and last, were the markings, natural or otherwise, guided by sacred forces?

"It is all three," the Being within the Stone answered. "All things work together to make beauty, to release the meaning of this world and the sacred. It is a holy collusion, and would that all find a stone that speaks to them. Draw close to your Stone and the powers revealed by it, for the Stone speaks of eternity."

"It has spoken," I concurred. "That a stone could harbor mystery and meaning, which does not seem to have an ending, is a surprise to me."

"Allow yourself to be surprised," said the Being. "For the mysteries are not over."

After that, the Being returned to deep within the stone, disappearing, and I surfaced to find the final Being I would encounter on the Stone.

CHAPTER THIRTEEN

The Flower World, indicated by the series of designs, dotted an expanse below me atop mountainous forms. The mountains shrugged and became the back of an animal. I was hurled from the matrix of the stone toward the head of this quadruped, which had a rayed eye. It was running or flying, a sacred deer messenger to the beyond, and it was taking me somewhere which would challenge any description in words. Rayed lights shot past me as I hurled toward a rising sun. They imbued the sky with shades of the rainbow, from bright green to a deep red. I was racing toward the origin of life, to the very first light. This ancient light was a different quality than the light we know. For it had a substance that refreshed one's being and bathed you as if it were liquid.

I knew this light was eternal and whatever bathed in it would also be eternal. whence this light came was unknowable, though we give varied names to it. For those who have experienced it, describe this feeling as being overwhelming and undeserved, and one which embraces opposites such that it is cool and refreshing, and warm and pulsing. This deer was racing that way as if to plunge wholesale into this origin being. It was baying a cry that reached into the heart of this ancient light which was also the future of all things.

I realized this was at the end of my journey, about, through, and above the Stone. It was time to put the stone back on a shelf, to wrap it in cloth and to save it for someone who would continue the journey. It was hard to let go, for the Stone promised continued discovery each time it was engaged. *How can it be endless?* I asked, as my last question. How could such richness be present in a common quartz cobblestone, more than a diamond or precious stone? The answer I knew was within me, one you will come to as well.

The End

Don't miss out!

Visit the website below and you can sign up to receive emails whenever Michael A. Susko publishes a new book. There's no charge and no obligation.

https://books2read.com/r/B-A-GJLJ-ATJXB

BOOKS 2 READ

Connecting independent readers to independent writers.

Did you love *Beyond the Portal: From Within the Mystery Stone*? Then you should read *Mystery Stone from the Shenandoah: Analyzed with Eastern Woodland Cosmology*[1] by Michael A. Susko!

[2]

A beautiful tablet-like mystery stone has been found by the Shenandoah River, near Berryville, Virginia. Underneath its brown-orange patina, peck-marked shapes reveal a crystalline heartstone underneath and intriguing designs. Varied opinions have been offered by experts on the oriign of the designs, so the author takes you on a tour of the stone so you can make your own judgement. He illustrates surprising gestalts, their aesthetic nature, and how they resonate with Eastern Woodland cosmology of early America. They include the presence of a pervasive spiritual energy, the tension and complementariness of twins, and forms which suggest the archetypes of avian-man, earth mother, and skeletal

1. https://books2read.com/u/b5XopA

2. https://books2read.com/u/b5XopA

shaman. With profuse images supported by commentary, we explore an alternative way to view the universe, and one that can enrich our lives.

Read more at https://www.allroneofus.com/.

Also by Michael A. Susko

A Couple Through Time
Down Below and the Archon's Castle
Up Above and the Runaway
Across the Gulf and Journey Into Un-Time
On the Bay and a Child Found
Down New River & Another World
In the Wild and Do One Wild Thing
On the Mountain and Two Are Missing
To the Beginning and Journey Through Here

Archetypal Worlds
Giant Under the Mountain
The Alien's Gift
The Gold People
Spider Woman and the Timeroc
Darkwood and Dual with the Shadow Side
Quill Ears & the Other Earth
Alwon in Another World: An Archetypal Voyage
Line In the Wall

Biographic Book of Tens
Ten Discoveries from Biology to Spirituality: Hidden & Life-Giving
Connections
Ten Times We Almost Died
Ten Sayings to Guide Our Lives
Ten Mystery Photos: Personal & Cosmological Reflections
Ten Mementos on Our Desk: Remembering Moments
Ten Metadiscoveries We Have Made

Haikus and Photos
Flowers and Haikus
Haikus and Photos: Guatemalan Highlands
Haikus and Photos: Water Birds and Reflections
Haikus and Photos: Seasons of New River
Haikus and Photos: Yosemite Wilderness
Haikus and Photos: California Coast
Haikus and Photos: Canadian Rockies
Haikus and Photos: Hawaii's Exotic Landscapes
Haikus and Photos: Vienna: People, Buildings and Art
Haikus and Photos: Slovakian Castles and Hamlets
Haikus and Photos: Berlin, Light and Dark
Haikus and Photos: New Orleans, City of Immigrants
Haikus and Photos: Antietam Wind and Spirits
Haikus & Photos: Plant Abstractions
Haikus and Photos: Appalachian Beauty
Haikus and Photos: Urban Farm in Sandtown
Haikus and Photos: New York Heights and Ground
Haikus & Photos: Santa Fe Fractal-Pueblo Spirtuality
Haikus and Photos: Monticello's Double Vision

Haikus and Photos: Presence at Penn Bluff
Haikus & Photos: Mystery Forms at Penn Bluff
Haikus and Photos: Essences at Penn Bluff
Haikus and Photos: World Archetypes at Penn Bluff

The Dreaming Series
Sleek Back
Streak and Cave Bear Dreaming
Moby and Marsupial Mole Dreaming

The Dream World Trilogy
Delphi, the Time Thief, and the Dream World
Detinna and the Cave God
The Resistance & the Empire

The Early Child
Child of the Elements
The New Ones

Transformational Stories
Caseness and Narrative: Contrasting Approaches to People
Psychiatrically Labeled
Transformative Experiences, Psychiatric Research, and Informed
Consent
Transformational Stories: Voices for True Healing in Mental Health

Writings from Street People
Street Images
Street Images II

Standalone
Little People & the Time-Rider
Animal Spell
The Firekeeper & Spirit of the Long Night
Ten Pulses of Evolution & the Surprising Nature of Evolutionary Time
Up Above and Down Below
Life's Dynamic Vulnerability: A Paradigm Shift in Biology
Alien Ally
The Generation of Life: Imagery, Ritual and Experiences in Deep Caves
Twelve Suspects
2084: Clash of Cults
Bats in the Future
Guard of the Dead
The Imagination Being
Ten Traits of Empire That Every Person Should Know
Aging and Renewal: Living the Full Life
The Meaning, Beauty & Mystery of Dreams: Seven Guidelines and
Seven Tools for Listening
The Fragility of Evolution: A Novel View
Ways We May Be Surprised by Heaven
Why Go Slow When You Can Hurl to Your Destruction!

About the Author

For many years, the author taught a course on the symbolism of Indigenous cultures. During several trips he made deep into the interior of Guatemala, he experienced the Indigenous lifestyle and was exposed to ancient Mayan rituals. In this work, he draws upon his experience as a photographer and his own vision quest experiences. By sharing this work, the author hopes to return the gift that this stone has given him.

Read more at https://www.allroneofus.com/.

About the Publisher

AllrOneofUs Publishing seeks out work which will make a novel and qualitative addition to the world literature, and one that will last across generations. Many of these persons are in the later part of their life and have made exemplary contributions which are unrecognized. To cite a few examples, we recommend Rich Mullin's *Ethics and the Full-breasted Richness of Life*, John Susko's *Flowers of the Night: Musings from a Sentimental Son,* and Dr. Curtis Adams' *Psychosis and the Humpty Dumpty Story.*

www.ingramcontent.com/pod-product-compliance
Lightning Source LLC
Chambersburg PA
CBHW021752150726
47989CB00004B/1618